Noah's Trees

Bijou Le Tord

HARPERCOLLINSPUBLISHERS

Noah's Trees
Copyright © 1999 by Bijou Le Tord
Printed in the U.S.A. All rights reserved.
http://www.harperchildrens.com

Library of Congress Cataloging-in-Publication Data
Le Tord, Bijou.
    Noah's trees / Bijou Le Tord.
        p.   cm.
    Summary: Noah nurtures his trees, planning to give them to his sons, but God has
another use for them in mind.
    ISBN 0-06-028235-5. — ISBN 0-06-028527-3 (lib. bdg.)
    1. Noah (Biblical figure)—Juvenile fiction.   [1. Noah (Biblical figure)—Fiction.
2. Trees—Fiction.]   I. Title.
PZ7.L568No 1999   98-53468
[E]—dc21   CIP
                                                                          AC

1   2   3   4   5   6   7   8   9   10
❖
First Edition

For

Julienne & John,

Rosie & Nips

and their families,

with love

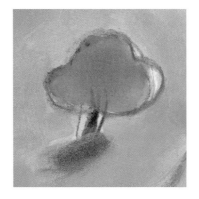

Noah loved God

and God

trusted him.

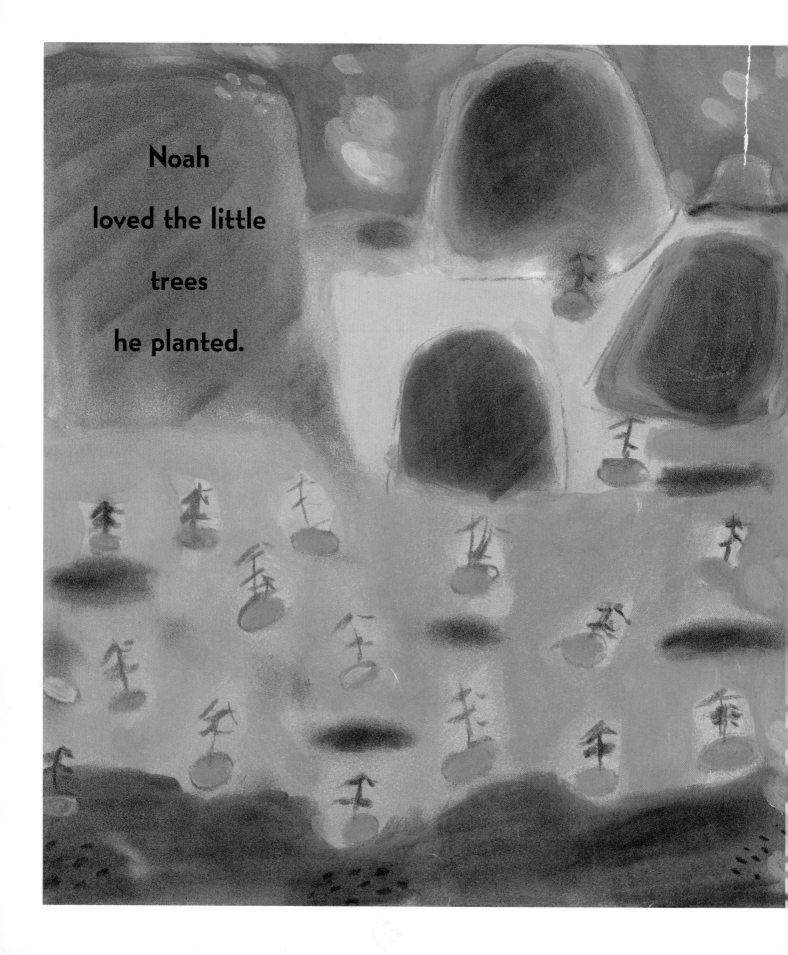

Noah
loved the little
trees
he planted.

He also loved

his three

sons.

He thought,

"One day

I will give them

my trees."

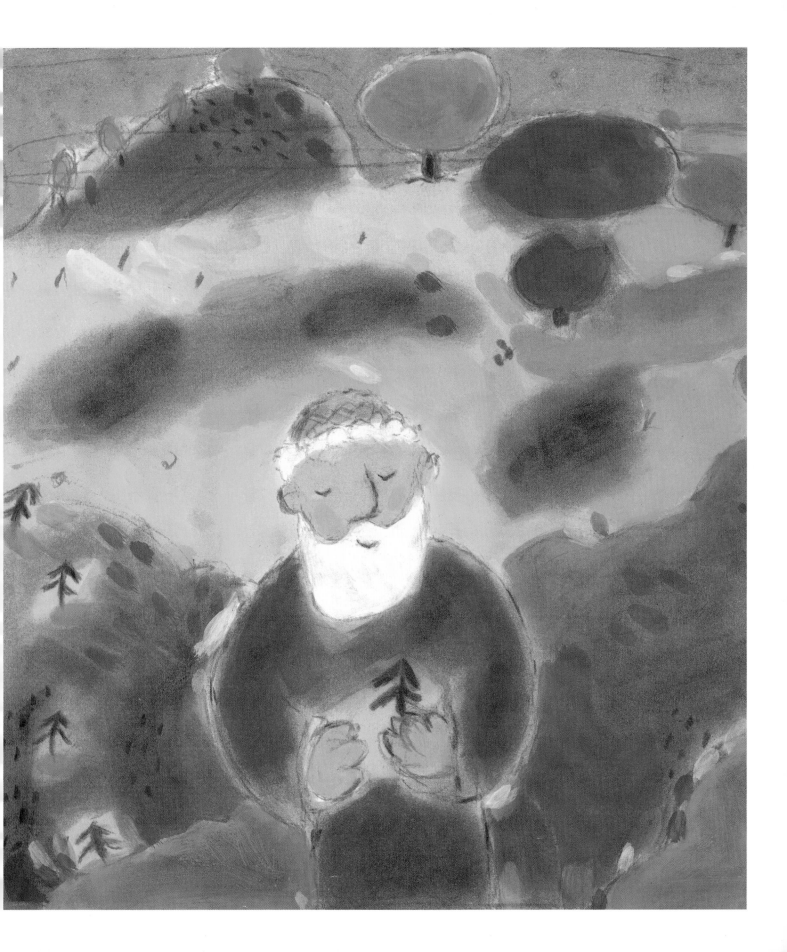

Noah

carefully watered

and weeded the ground

around the tiny trees.

He pruned

and snipped

and watched them grow.

In winter

he protected them

with straw.

And sometimes, like a true gardener, he spoke to them in a soft voice.

In time
the trees grew
strong branches
and their leaves
rustled in the
wind.

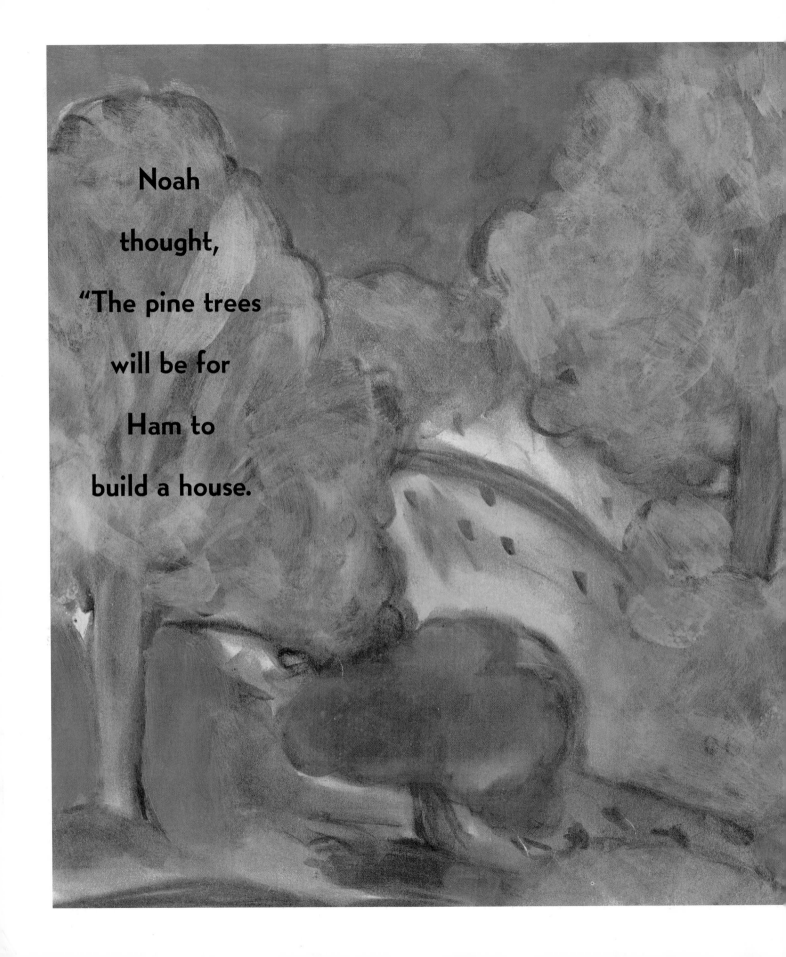

Noah thought, "The pine trees will be for Ham to build a house.

The oaks are
for Shem,
and he
can carve
a cradle
for his
daughter."

"Japheth will make a flute out of the fruit trees.

With his baby he'll watch the branches fill with birds."

Noah was happy.
The trees
became
a great forest.

He could
smell their
beautiful tree
scent.

Then,

one day

God said to Noah,

"I will make

a great flood.

Build an ark

for you, your family,

and the animals.

Make it out of

your favorite trees."

Noah listened

to God

quietly.

He touched

the rough, warm bark

of the oaks, the pines,

and the fruit trees.

And he said

good-bye.

Then,

he set to work.

He took

his axe and

his saw

and felled

all the trees

to the ground.

He didn't stop

his work

until the ark

was finished.

Noah

prepared for

sailing.

And

two by two

the animals

came in.

He carried

into the ark

little green saplings

from

the trees

he loved the most.

Just then,

the sun

hid behind the

clouds.

And it began

to rain.